Dear Parent:

Your child's love of reading starts here!

Every child learns to read in a different way and at his or her own speed. Some go back and forth between reading levels and read favorite books again and again. Others read through each level in order. You can help your young reader improve and become more confident by encouraging his or her own interests and abilities. From books your child reads with you to the first books he or she reads alone, there are I Can Read Books for every stage of reading:

SHARED READING
My First

Basic language, word repetition, and whimsical illustrations, ideal for sharing with your emergent reader

MAR   2020

BEGINNING READING
1

Short sentences, familiar words, and simple concepts for children eager to read on their own

READING WITH HELP
2

Engaging stories, longer sentences, and language play for developing readers

READING ALONE
3

Complex plots, challenging vocabulary, and high-interest topics for the independent reader

I Can Read Books have introduced children to the joy of reading since 1957. Featuring award-winning authors and illustrators and a fabulous cast of beloved characters, I Can Read Books set the standard for beginning readers.

A lifetime of discovery begins with the magical words "I Can Read!"

Visit www.icanread.com for information
on enriching your child's reading experience.

Funding for MOLLY OF DENALI is provided by the Corporation for Public Broadcasting and by public television viewers. In addition, the contents of MOLLY OF DENALI were developed under a grant from the Department of Education. However, those contents do not necessarily represent the policy of the Department of Education, and you should not assume endorsement by the Federal Government. The project is funded by a Ready To Learn grant (PR/AWARD No. U295A150003, CFDA No. 84.295A).

www.icanread.com

ISBN 978-0-06-295034-5

Book design by Brenda E. Angelilli and Marisa Rother

19 20 21 22 23 LSCC 10 9 8 7 6 5 4 3 2 1 ❖ First Edition

I Can Read!

BEGINNING 1 READING

MOLLY of DENALI™

Party Moose

Based on a television
episode written by
Kathy Waugh

HARPER
An Imprint of HarperCollinsPublishers

Hey, everyone, it's Molly!
Today I have a surprise
for my friend Nina.

It's Nina's birthday!

I made her a party box

filled with noisemakers,

hats, and horns.

5

For an extra birthday gift,
I got Nina a book
called *One Thousand Fixes*
for Outdoor Mishaps.

"How are you going to get
the box to Nina?" asks Trini.
Nina is up north
filming caribou with her team.
Nina is a nature journalist.

"My mom is flying her plane up
to deliver supplies to Nina's team.
I'm going to ride up with Mom
and surprise Nina!" I say.

"My gift is a spruce cone!" says Trini.

"I made a whistle out of wood,"

says Tooey.

It's super loud!

I put the gifts in the box.

It's almost time to leave!

A little later, Mom and I take off.

I look out the plane window.

"Look, Mom!" I say.

"I see *vadzaih*—caribou!"

"It's always special to see *vadzaih*,"
says Mom.

Soon it's time to land.

"But what's that?" Mom asks,

pointing at the runway.

Something big and black is below.

"Maybe it's a rock," I say.

I take out binoculars

for a closer look.

"It's a gigantic moose!" I shout.

"He's eating something."

"I'll circle the runway.

The noise will scare him off,"

Mom says.

But the moose ignores the airplane.

He's eating berries off a bush.

He doesn't want to move!

"I'll call Nina and ask if her team
can come to the runway
to help us," Mom says.

"I'll circle the runway.

The noise will scare him off,"

Mom says.

But the moose ignores the airplane.

He's eating berries off a bush.

He doesn't want to move!

"I'll call Nina and ask if her team
can come to the runway
to help us," Mom says.

"Don't say I'm here!" I say.

"It's supposed to be a surprise!"

Mom promises not to say a word.

Nina and her team come right away.

"Shoo, moose!" they all yell.

The moose moves . . .

but only one bush over.

He is still on the runway.

Nina calls Mom.

"We're not sure what else to do.

He's not budging," Nina says.

"If I can't land in ten minutes,
I'll have to turn around," says Mom.
"I need plenty of gas to get home."

If the moose won't leave,

Mom will have to air-drop supplies.

That means Mom drops supplies

while the plane is in the air.

But what about my big surprise?

"There must be something we can do!"

I say.

I unwrap Nina's birthday gift,

the book called *One Thousand Fixes*

for Outdoor Mishaps.

Maybe there is a fix

for getting a moose to move!

I check the book index

for the word "moose."

There is a chapter about

how to safely move a moose.

"That's what we need!" I say.

I flip to the right page.

"How to move a moose:

make a ruckus from a safe distance."

I look at the picture in the book

of people making noise.

Ruckus must mean noise!

Nina's shouting

hadn't been loud enough.

"My party box is full of noise!"

I say.

"Can we drop it for Nina?"

Mom calls Nina to tell her the plan.

"Molly remembered my birthday!"

Nina says when she sees the box.

She takes out the noisemakers.

Nina and her team start to make lots and lots of noise.

Nina even uses the wooden whistle that Tooey made for her.

It makes a very loud sound.

The sound startles the moose!

The moose runs back into the wild.

Everyone cheers.

After the plane lands safely,

I hide in the back behind the cargo.

"Good job!" Nina says.

"All thanks to you, Nina!" says Mom.

"And a certain other person . . ."

I jump out from the plane.

"Surprise!" I yell.

Nina looks so happy she could cry.

She gives me a big hug.

It is time to celebrate!

Everyone sings a song.

"Happy birthday to you,
happy birthday to you,
we almost missed it,
but our Molly came through!"

Molly's Guide on How to Make Your Own Party Box!

A party box is exactly what it sounds like—all the items you need to have an awesome party, right in a box! Party boxes are a great way to celebrate birthdays and other special occasions. That's because when you open a party box, the party comes to you!

Here's how to make one:

- **First, grab a box!** Any kind of box will work, it just needs to be big enough to hold all your party items.
- **Next, decorate your box.** You can use stickers, markers, glitter, and bows.
- **Fill up the box with party supplies**—like streamers, balloons, and party hats!
- **Next, add noisemakers to the party box!** It's just not a party without lots of ways to celebrate and make some noise!
- **If you are giving your party box to someone** to celebrate a special occasion, you might want to add an extra special gift just for them. A handmade card or a gift that you found in nature is a good way to let the person know how much you care!
- **Top it off with CONFETTI!** A party box isn't complete without confetti!

Most important: Have lots and lots of FUN making it!